I Am a
SKATER

As photographed by Jane Feldman

Random House 🏠 New York

To Lena, Kalina, Ayannah, Chamisa, Kelsey, Sarah, Tyson, Jannelle, Grayson, Phoebe, Ali, James Patrick, Michaelangelo, Emily, Alex, Katya, and McKenzie—the youngest dreamers of my extended family. They are my most constructive critics and surround me with constant inspiration. And, of course, to the dreamer in us all!

Text and all photographs, including back cover, copyright © 2002 by Jane Feldman,
with the exception of p. 16 bottom left, p. 18 top left, p. 19 bottom right, © 2000 by Bob Ewell;
p. 10 top, courtesy of Denis Nicholson; p. 10 bottom, courtesy of David and Linda Karp; p. 11 top right, © Duomo/CORBIS;
p. 29 top left, courtesy of Andrew Pastarnack; and additional childhood pictures, courtesy of the Hughes family.
All rights reserved under International and Pan-American Copyright Conventions.
Published in the United States by Random House, Inc., New York,
and simultaneously in Canada by Random House of Canada Limited, Toronto.

www.randomhouse.com/kids

Library of Congress Cataloging-in-Publication Data
Feldman, Jane.
I am a skater / as photographed by Jane Feldman. p. cm. — (Young dreamers)
ISBN 0-375-80256-8 (trade) — ISBN 0-375-90256-2 (lib. bdg.)   1. Hughes, Emily, 1989– —Juvenile literature.
2. Hughes, Emily, 1989– —Pictorial works—Juvenile literature. 3. Skaters—United States—Biography—Juvenile literature.
[1. Hughes, Emily, 1989– 2. Ice skaters. 3. Women—Biography.]
I. Title. II. Series. GV850.H85 A3 2002   796.91'092—dc21   [B]   2001019977

Printed in the United States of America First Edition January 2002 10 9 8 7 6 5 4 3 2
RANDOM HOUSE and colophon are registered trademarks of Random House, Inc.

This book came to be as a huge collaborative effort. First, I would like to thank Emily Hughes for her enthusiasm, patience, and thoughtfulness, as well as the entire Hughes family—Amy, John, Rebecca, David, Matt, Sarah, and Taylor—for their extraordinary support. I would like to thank Jo Jo Starbuck for introducing me to the Hughes family and Wendy Hilliard for introducing me to Jo Jo.

I would also like to acknowledge Bonni Retzkin, Emily's coach and extended-family member, for her patience, guidance, and enthusiasm; Debbie Starkman and Lauren Jason; Patricia (Tricia) O'Donnell, for her work with us in both Pilates and ballet; Linda Cozzi and Dana Heckler, whose costumes were an inspiration; and the Klingbeil family.

Thanks to the Ice Rink at Rockefeller Center, Madison Square Garden and the New York Rangers, Wollman Rink/the Makkos Organization, Sid Morgan at Chelsea Piers, Parkwood Ice Rink, and Kim Bennett and Rick Gardner at Newbridge Arena for providing us with the ultimate locations to photograph.

I would like to extend my gratitude to the extraordinary Champions on Ice®: Michelle Kwan, Brian Boitano, Todd Eldredge, Elvis Stojko (and his coach, Uschi Keszler), Philippe Candeloro, Surya Bonaly, Rudy Galindo, Evgeny Plushenko, Irina Slutskaya, and, of course, Sarah Hughes for their contributions. I would also like to thank Tom Collins and Lynn Plage at Champions on Ice® for their support of this book and for bringing the world's greatest skaters to so many live audiences throughout the country.

To Anastasia "Nastia" Gromova and Chloe Nelson for their skating contributions. To the amazing staff at Random House, especially Shana Corey, Michael Caputo, Jason Zamajtuk, Gail Smith, Diane Landolf, Kate Klimo, and Mallory Loehr.

To Rob, Darvin, and the rest of the gang at FotoCare for their TLC, and to Westside Color. To my CityKids Foundation and Darrow School families. To my extended and nuclear family.

And to the Creator—the source of all creativity.

Hi! My name is Emily Hughes.
I'm twelve years old, and I am a skater.

$\mathcal{I}$'ve been ice-skating for as long as I can remember. I'm the second youngest of six kids and we all skate. My dad got us started. He played hockey at Cornell University and tried out for the Toronto Maple Leafs.

Here I am with my older brothers and sisters when I was two years old. My younger sister, Taylor, wasn't born yet.

I used to tag along with my big sister Sarah when she went skating. She made it look like so much fun!

Here's me, Taylor, and Sarah with Olympic champion Jo Jo Starbuck. Jo Jo used to work with Sarah.

Nowadays, Sarah's an Olympic gold medalist–proof that dreams can come true!

My mom's the only one in the family who doesn't skate, but she still manages to keep up with us. Actually, the rest of us usually have trouble keeping up with *her*!

My whole family now (there are a lot of us!).

Mom

Me

Taylor

Matt

Sarah

David

Rebecca

Dad

This is Taylor's and my room. It used to be Rebecca's before we started adding more bedrooms to the house, then it was Sarah's, and now it's ours. I don't spend much time here, though—I'm usually on the go!

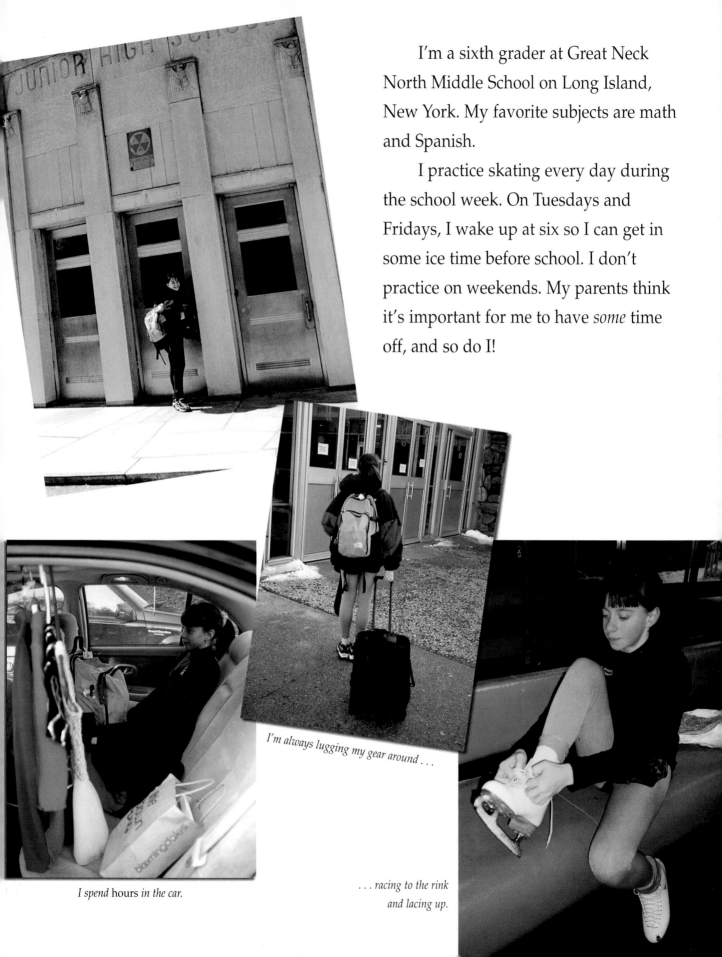

I'm a sixth grader at Great Neck North Middle School on Long Island, New York. My favorite subjects are math and Spanish.

I practice skating every day during the school week. On Tuesdays and Fridays, I wake up at six so I can get in some ice time before school. I don't practice on weekends. My parents think it's important for me to have *some* time off, and so do I!

I'm always lugging my gear around . . .

I spend hours in the car.

. . . racing to the rink and lacing up.

Me and Bonnie then.

ℳy coach, Bonni Retzkin, works with me when I practice and travels with me when I go out of town to compete or perform. She's been my coach since I was four and is almost a second mom to me.

Bonni says the most important thing about skating is to have fun and be happy.

Bonni's dog, Buddy, is our mascot!

Me and Bonnie now.

Bonni always makes sure
I start with stretches. Stretching
warms up my muscles and helps
prevent injuries.

After I stretch, I hit the ice.
It's cold at first, but once I start
moving, I warm up pretty
quickly.

My favorite moves are jumps and spins. When I start learning a jump, I wear a harness. The harness is attached to a cable that runs across the rink. It helps me stay in the air long enough to complete the full jump and then cushions my landing until I'm able to do it myself. Once I've learned a jump and the harness is off, I feel like I'm flying!

In a headless scratch spin, your head is so far back that people watching can hardly see it.

In an outside spread eagle, you lean back on the edge of your skates.

This is called a falling leaf.

Right now I'm working on a new program about the Olympics. In the program, I act out being an Olympic ice hockey player, a skier, and, of course, a figure skater. This routine is really cool because I wear three different costumes and have lots of props. The hardest prop to work with is the flag. It's *so* heavy!

When Bonni and I practice, we spend a lot of time working on different moves.

A lot of moves are named after the skater who created them. This is a Bielmann. It's my favorite move because it's very challenging.

I think this camel spin is fine, but Bonni says that I should arch my back more and hold my head up.

I made this up myself! I call it a Malistar.

Bonni likes my spiral because she says I have good extension. "Extension" means how high your leg is and how complete the stretch is.

This is a pull-up-the-blade spin. See how stretching can pay off?

The butterfly is one of the hardest jumps because at one point both of your legs have to go higher than your head!

This is called a layback because you "lay back" and look at the ceiling.

When you take off into a lutz jump, you start by skating backward.

The shoot-the-duck sit spin is another one of my favorites because I've been doing it since I was little.

Of course, not everything about skating is fun. Part of skating is falling, and when you skate as much as I do, you fall *a lot*. I'm so used to falling now that I hardly ever cry, but I don't think falling *or* crying is anything to be ashamed of. The important thing is having the courage to get back up again.

A few years ago, I had a very bad fall. I shattered my ankle, and the doctors thought my skating days were over. But I don't give up easily. Six months later, I was back on the ice!

$\mathcal{B}$elieve it or not, there's a lot to skating that happens outside of the rink. I take Pilates lessons to help develop my strength and flexibility. Pilates is a form of exercise developed for ballet dancers that a lot of athletes—and non-athletes—do, too!

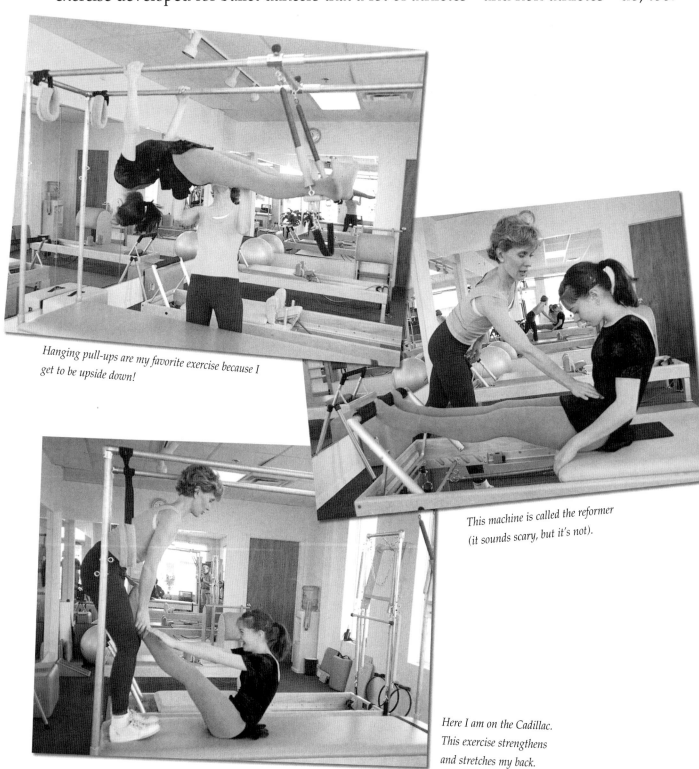

Hanging pull-ups are my favorite exercise because I get to be upside down!

This machine is called the reformer (it sounds scary, but it's not).

Here I am on the Cadillac. This exercise strengthens and stretches my back.

I also take ballet. Ballet helps with my extension and teaches me to be graceful on the ice.

I play violin, too, because understanding music helps me with the choreography and timing of my skating programs. Bonni picks the music for my routines. She looks for something that matches my personality—it has to have a lot of energy! Then we listen to it together to see if we like it.

As you can see, I'm always in my skating dress because there's never any time to change!

Even with Pilates and ballet and violin, I find time to go back to the rink for a skating lesson after school. The rink is my home away from home.

I met my best friend, Lauren, at the rink.

Lauren, me, our friend Jessica, and my little sister, Taylor, practicing a group routine.

I even had my twelfth-birthday party at the rink!

Bonni and Chloe work on spirals!

Chloe's seven and she's really fun to skate with.

$\mathcal{B}$onni doesn't coach just me in skating. She works with other kids, too. Lately, she's been showing me how to work with younger skaters. When we teach a skater something new, we show her how to position herself and how the correct form should feel, so that she'll be able to do it on her own.

The important thing about sit spins is to get as low as possible.

Chloe shows me her scratch spin.

Chloe is always willing to try something new!

I like skating with younger kids because I remember how much older skaters' encouragement always meant to me when I was little. It still means a lot! Nastia is five years old. Her parents used to skate competitively in Russia; now they both coach at the rink that I go to.

Nastia just won her first trophy!

A lot of little kids' routines end with curtsies.

I've been competing since I was even younger than Nastia. This year, I had my first international competition! It was in Denmark. My mom and Bonni went with me and we got to meet skaters from all over the world.

I won my first trophy when I was four.

I won my first medal when I was six.

$\mathcal{I}$ like competing, but I think performing's even more exciting. When you perform, you can share the joy you get from skating with everyone in the audience.

My family recently went to see Sarah skate with Champions on Ice®. I watch Sarah skate all the time, but seeing her in front of all those people, along with some of the world's greatest skaters, gave me goose bumps.

Having a champion for a sister has its perks. After the show, we went backstage and I got to meet some of my heroes *in person*! They were so encouraging!

My sister, the champion!

Me with Brian Boitano.

Me and Rudy Galindo.

Irina Slutskaya and Sarah. (Sarah loved her costume!)

Sarah with Evgeny Plushenko. Check out this *costume!*

Me with Todd Eldredge.

Sarah with Surya Bonaly. (Everyone hams it up backstage.)

Elvis Stojko with his coach, Uschi Keszler, and me.

Here's me and Taylor with Philippe Candeloro.

Me with Sarah and Michelle Kwan—what a thrill! On a skating tour, everyone starts to feel like family.

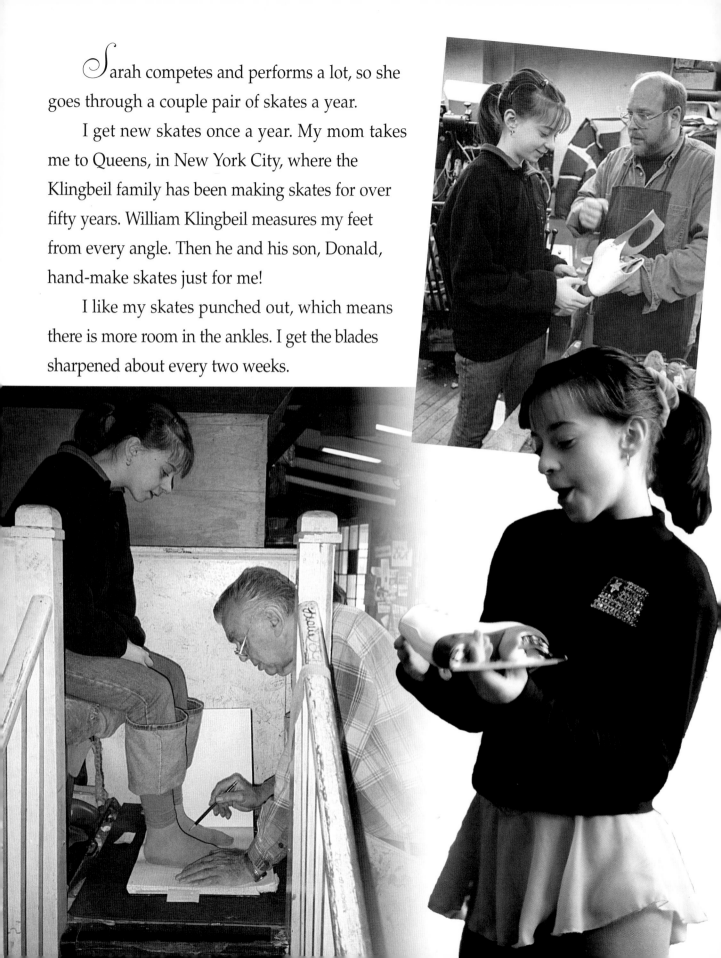

Sarah competes and performs a lot, so she goes through a couple pair of skates a year.

I get new skates once a year. My mom takes me to Queens, in New York City, where the Klingbeil family has been making skates for over fifty years. William Klingbeil measures my feet from every angle. Then he and his son, Donald, hand-make skates just for me!

I like my skates punched out, which means there is more room in the ankles. I get the blades sharpened about every two weeks.

When I'm getting ready for a new performance or a competition, I go see Linda Cozzi, who makes skating costumes. Linda watches me skate and then designs an outfit to match the mood of my routine. When I practice, I wear Sarah's old skating dresses.

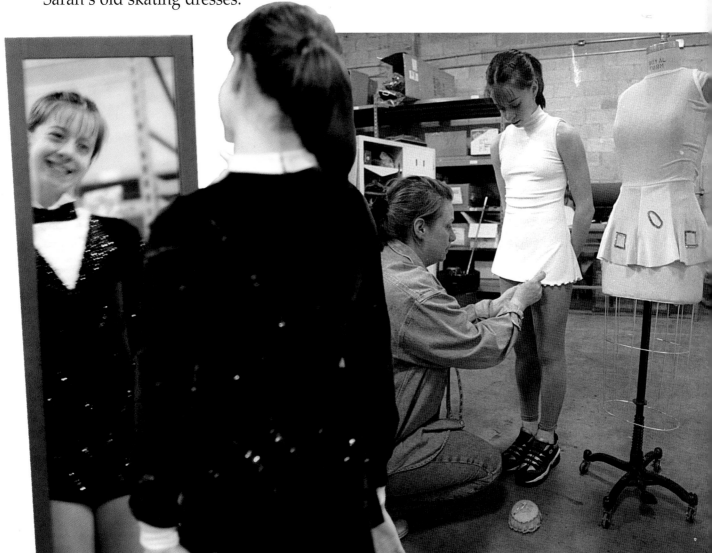

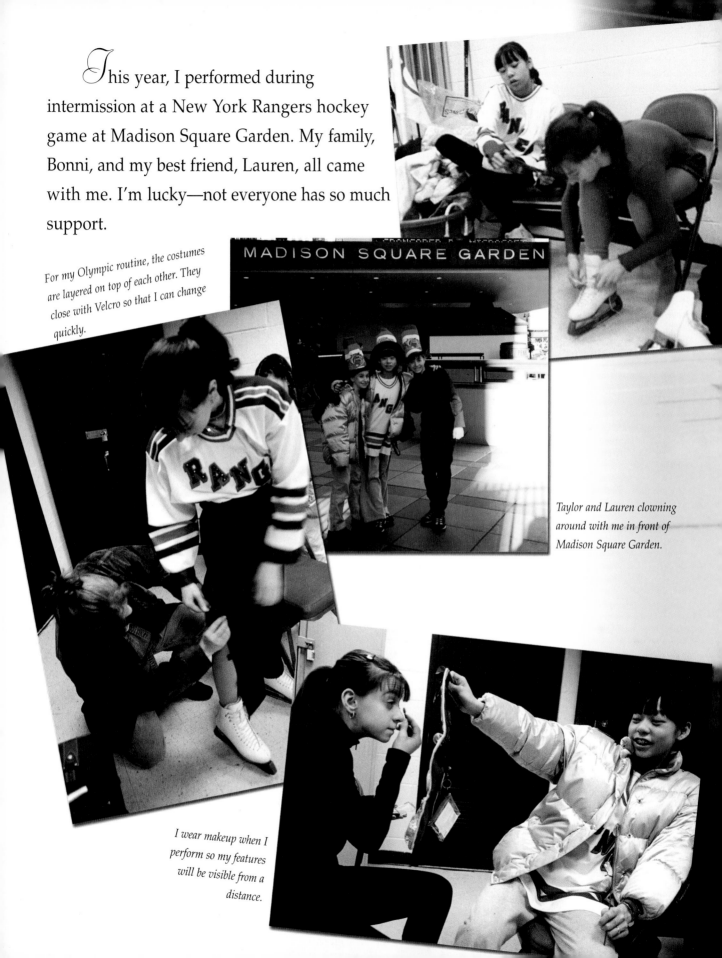

𝒯his year, I performed during intermission at a New York Rangers hockey game at Madison Square Garden. My family, Bonni, and my best friend, Lauren, all came with me. I'm lucky—not everyone has so much support.

For my Olympic routine, the costumes are layered on top of each other. They close with Velcro so that I can change quickly.

MADISON SQUARE GARDEN

Taylor and Lauren clowning around with me in front of Madison Square Garden.

I wear makeup when I perform so my features will be visible from a distance.

The Rangers game was sold out,
which meant almost 20,000 people
were going to be watching me! I tried
not to think about it. I just pictured
what I was going to do in my program
and concentrated on that.

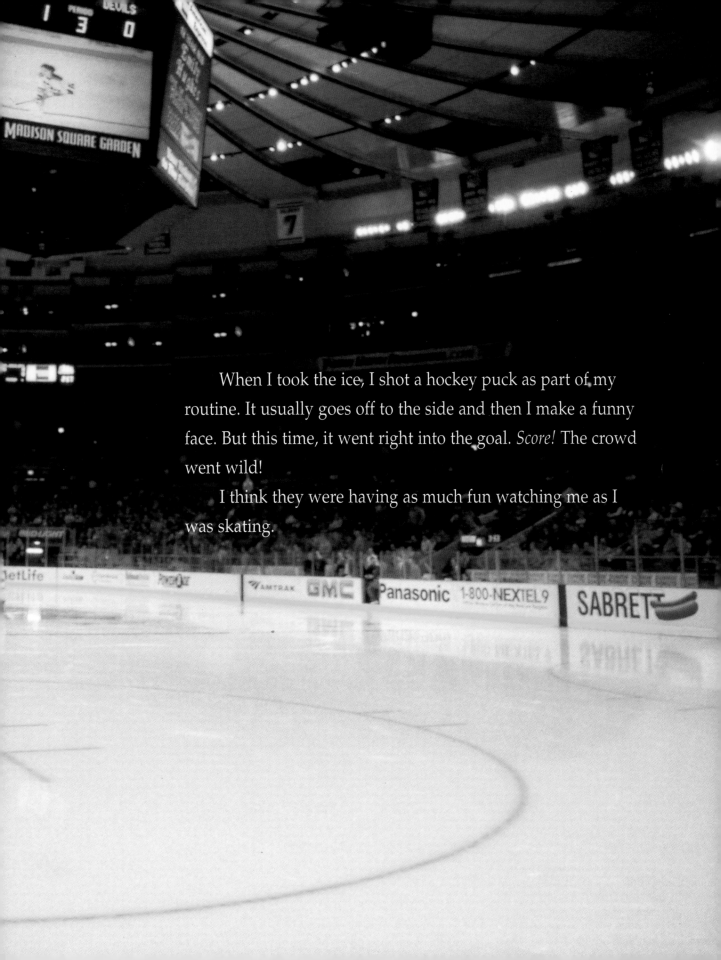

When I took the ice, I shot a hockey puck as part of my routine. It usually goes off to the side and then I make a funny face. But this time, it went right into the goal. *Score!* The crowd went wild!

I think they were having as much fun watching me as I was skating.

My family and Bonni were cheering
me on, too, which made it even better.

Bonni never stops coaching!

Lauren came right out on the ice to help
me with all my props.

This is me pretending to be an Olympic skier—I guess it's a little
different when you're on a mountain!

I was so happy I managed the flag!

It's at moments like these—when all the practice, lessons, falls, and hard work come together at once—that I know as much as I put into skating, I get even more back.

$\mathcal{I}$'m not sure if professional skating is in my future. But I
do know that wherever I am and whatever I end up doing . . .

. . . *I'll always be a skater!*

*J*ane Feldman is a professional photographer whose striking work has gained international attention in the field of advertising and among nonprofit organizations that promote youth empowerment. This is Ms. Feldman's fourth book in the Young Dreamers series. She is also the coauthor and photographer of *Jefferson's Children: The Story of One American Family*, an ALA Best Book for Young Adults. A native New Yorker, Ms. Feldman divides her time between Manhattan and the Berkshire Mountains in Massachusetts.